Andy and the Runaway Horse

Jane Thayer

Illustrated by Meg Wohlberg

William Morrow & Company

New York • 1963

Published simultaneously in the Dominion of
Canada by George J. McLeod Limited, Toronto.

Printed in the United States of America.

BY AMERICAN BOOK-STRATFORD PRESS INC., N.Y.

Library of Congress Catalog Card Number 63-7879

Weekly Reader Book Club Edition

One day Andy was walking down Main Street when he stopped and stared.

He had seen pictures of
horses in books, but he had
never seen one in real life.

"What's that?" cried Andy,
just to make sure.

"For goodness sake! That's a horse pulling a junk wagon," said Mother. "I haven't seen that since I was a little girl!"

The horse was trotting down Main Street with the cars and trucks, while the bells on the junk wagon jingled. As he came to where Andy and Mother were standing, he slowed down. He came up to the curb. He walked past a

sign that said, *No Parking,* and
parked at a parking meter.

The junkman, whose name was Mr. Donkersloot, put a nickel in the meter.

"Is that your horse?" said Andy.

"Yes," said Mr. Donkersloot.

"What's his name?" said Andy.

"Alice," said Mr. Donker-sloot.

"How come you have a horse instead of a truck?" said Andy.

"Truck broke down," said Mr. Donkersloot. "I brought Alice to town, and she gets along fine in traffic. So what do I need with a truck?"

"Horses are better," said Andy.

"Sure, when they're as smart as this one," said Mr. Donkersloot.

Andy watched Mr. Don-
kersloot give Alice a bag of
oats. He watched him climb

back into the wagon to eat a
liverwurst sandwich and drink
a cup of coffee.

"Know why that horse is parked there?" said Andy to Mother.

"So she can eat her oats," said Mother.

"Because she has to park at a parking meter," Andy explained.

"Oh yes, of course," said Mother.

"Everybody has to park at a parking meter," Andy explained to Mother.

Alice the horse looked at
Andy, as she calmly munched
her oats, and said (so no one
else could hear) that he was a
bright boy.

Andy and Mother went on,
and stopped at some stores.
They walked along Main
Street. Andy looked at the
cars and trucks whizzing by.

Suddenly he heard jingling bells again. Alice the horse had finished her oats, and here she came trotting along with all the cars and trucks.

Just then the traffic lights
turned red. The cars and the
trucks stopped. Alice the horse
stopped also.

"Know why that horse stopped?" said Andy to Mother.

"Mr. Donkersloot pulled the reins," said Mother.

"Because the light turned red," Andy explained.

"Oh yes, of course," said Mother.

"Everybody has to stop at a red light," Andy explained to Mother.

Andy and Mother came to the corner of Main and Maple Streets. They decided to cross Main Street. The traffic light was red for Maple, but it was green for Main Street. The cars and trucks came whizzing by. Andy and Mother waited, but the lights did not change.

A man came along. He didn't wait for the lights to

change. He walked right up to
a pole and pressed a button.

The lights changed! The cars and trucks on Main Street stopped. Alice the horse was coming along, and she stopped too. The man crossed Main Street, and so did Andy and Mother.

Andy was so surprised that he said to the man, "Did you make the lights change?"

"Yes," said the man.

"How?" said Andy.

"I pressed the button," said the man.

"At this corner," explained the man, "the light is always green for Main Street unless someone wants to cross. If you want to cross Main Street, you press the button. The lights change long enough to let you get across."

"I want to make the lights change!" cried Andy.

"Tomorrow," said Mother.

So the next day Andy and Mother went to the corner of Main and Maple again. The cars and trucks came whizzing by. Andy did not waste a moment. He ran to the pole. He stood on tiptoe and pressed the button.

The lights changed! The
cars and trucks stopped. Andy
and Mother crossed the street
while the cars and the trucks
waited. Andy was simply de-
lighted.

After that, whenever Andy went shopping with Mother on Main Street, he did two things. He had a talk with Alice the horse if she happened to be parked some place. And he made the lights change at Main and Maple.

One day Andy was walking down Main Street, quite near Maple, when suddenly, somewhere, there was a loud *Bang.* Andy jumped, he was so startled. "What's that?" he cried.

"That was just a car backfiring," Mother explained.

Up the street, Alice the horse was calmly munching her oats when she heard the loud *Bang* too. Alice the horse jumped, she was so startled. What's that? she thought.

No one told her it was just a car backfiring. Alice the horse was so scared she leaped and pawed the air. Mr. Donkersloot's coffee flew out of his hand. With a snort and a clatter, Alice started down Main Street.

All the people, including Andy, looked up Main Street and saw Alice coming, with the junk wagon rattling and the bells jinglejangling.

Mr. Donkersloot pulled the reins, but he couldn't stop Alice.

A policeman whistled. He couldn't stop Alice.

"Oh, stop that runaway horse!" cried a lady.

"How can we stop her?" everyone cried.

Then Andy knew just what to do. Down Main Street he ran toward the corner of Main and Maple, as fast as his legs would go. He rushed to the pole. He stood on tiptoe. He pressed the button.

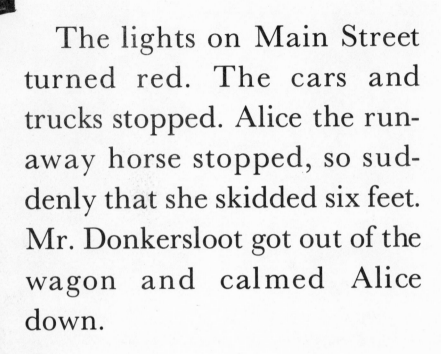

The lights on Main Street turned red. The cars and trucks stopped. Alice the runaway horse stopped, so suddenly that she skidded six feet. Mr. Donkersloot got out of the wagon and calmed Alice down.

All the people who were watching the runaway horse were amazed. They said to Andy, "Oh! Do horses always stop at red lights?"

"Sure they do. Everybody stops at a red light," explained Andy.

Then Mr. Donkersloot shook hands with Andy and said, "Thank you!"

The policeman praised him.

A lady kissed him.

Mother was proud as Punch.

Andy explained to Alice the loud bang was just a car back-firing.

Alice looked a little ashamed of herself for running away. But she told Andy (in private when no one was listening), it certainly was a good thing *someone* was around who understood about red lights!